The Race for the
Chinese Zodiac

For Emma and Jack, our little Rooster and Rat
G. W.

For Lauris and her amazing crew — with thanks
S. R.

First U.S. edition 2013

Library of Congress Catalog Card Number 2012950621
ISBN 978-0-7636-6778-8

13 14 15 16 17 18 SCP 10 9 8 7 6 5 4 3 2 1

Printed in Humen, Dongguan, China

This book was typeset in Chaparral.
The illustrations were done in Chinese ink, linocuts, and digital media.

Candlewick Press
99 Dover Street
Somerville, Massachusetts 02144

visit us at www.candlewick.com

The Race for the
Chinese Zodiac

Gabrielle Wang

illustrated by

Sally Rippin

CANDLEWICK PRESS

Long ago in ancient China, the Jade Emperor,
who was ruler of Heaven and Earth,
proclaimed a mighty race.
"The first twelve animals to cross the river
will each have a year named after them,"
he announced.

The animals lined up along the shore,
eager to begin.
The waters slapped and swirled.
The mountains trembled.
The Jade Emperor's gong rang out.

Courageous Tiger leaped into the river, striking out with his powerful paws.

Peaceful Rabbit jumped onto a log,
holding on with all her might.

Charming Rat and Friendly Cat were very good friends. They did everything together. "Take us across on your back, Ox, and we will show you the way." Kind Ox agreed and they climbed on board.

Faithful Dog played in the shallows,
jumping and splashing and chasing his shadow.

Lucky Rooster found a raft.
"Who will give me a hand?" he asked.
"I will," said Clever Monkey, and he cleared
away the reeds. Then Gentle Goat pushed the
raft into the water.

Spirited Horse plunged into the river,
hooves churning up mud from the riverbed.
But who was hiding in Horse's mane?
It was Wise Snake, getting a free ride!

Happy Pig put her toe in the water,
then drew it out again. "I'm hungry.
I need something to eat," she said.
So Pig ate and ate and ate until her
tummy was as

big as a balloon.

Then she fell asleep in the mud.

Powerful Dragon flew out
across the river, scales shimmering
like pearls in the sun.
The clouds parted. Thunder rumbled,
shaking the mountaintops.

"We're winning!" cried Rat.
When Cat stood up to look,
Rat pushed her into the water.

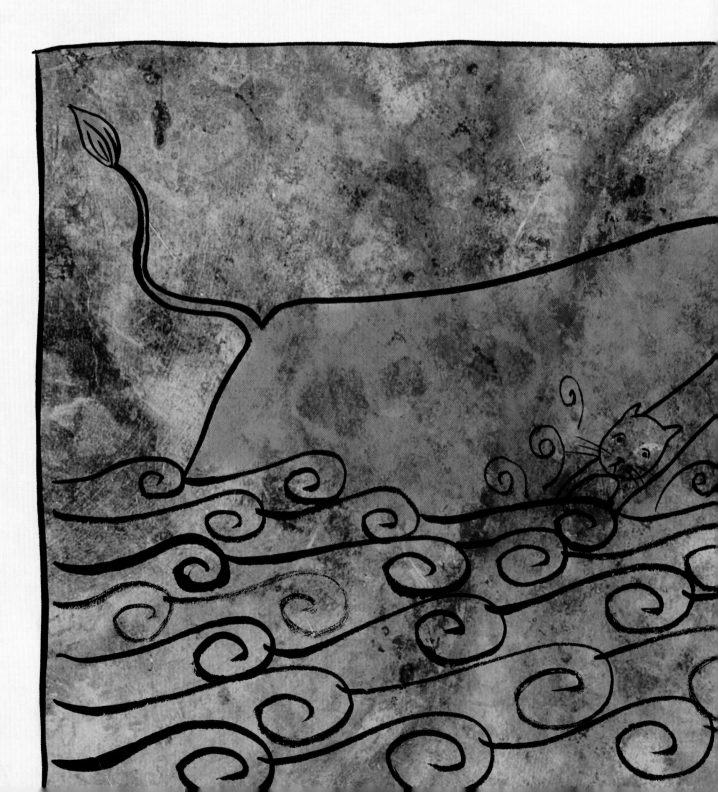

"What was that?" Ox asked.
"Oh, nothing," Rat replied.
  Rat would do anything to come in first.

As Ox dragged herself onto the bank,
Rat leaped across the finish line.

"The first year will be named
after you, Rat," the Jade Emperor declared.
"And the second year after Ox."

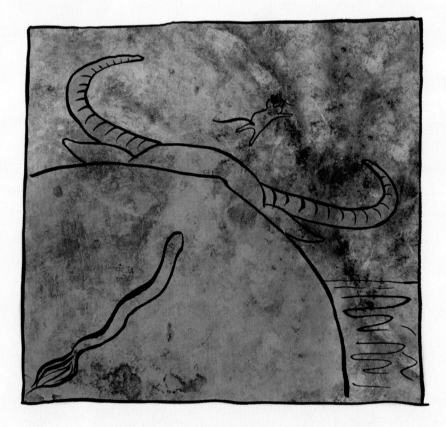

"Why so slow, Tiger?" Rabbit called out.
"I was carried downstream on
 a strong current," Tiger replied.
"But I'm back on course now!"

Just then, a breath of wind blew Rabbit
all the way to shore.
She leaped off her log and hopped
across the finish line, right behind Tiger.

Next came Dragon, swooping down
from the sky. "What held you up?"
the Jade Emperor asked.
"I saw people and animals suffering
a terrible drought, so I stopped
to make rain," Dragon replied.

"Then I saw a poor little rabbit clinging to a log and blew her to the shore."
"You have a kind heart," the Jade Emperor said. "The fifth year of the zodiac will be named after you."

Horse galloped toward the finish line. *I'm next,* she thought. But at the last second, Snake sprang to the ground, beating Horse by a flicker of his tongue.

Goat, Monkey, and Rooster jumped off their raft. "You three work well together," the Jade Emperor said. "The eighth, ninth, and tenth years will be the Years of the Goat, Monkey, and Rooster."

Dog dashed toward the emperor, wagging his stumpy tail. "I was playing in the shallows and almost forgot the race," he barked.

The Jade Emperor smiled. "The eleventh year will be named after you, little dog."

After waking from a long nap, Pig floated across on her tummy.

"You have done well, too," the Jade Emperor said. "And so, the final spot on the zodiac belongs to you."

Poor Cat dragged herself up onto the bank.
But she was too late. There are only twelve
places on the Chinese zodiac.

And that is why, to this very day,
cats have hated rats.

The Twelve Animals of the Chinese Zodiac

Rat: 1924, 1936, 1948, 1960, 1972, 1984, 1996, 2008, 2020, 2032
Those born in the year of the Rat are intelligent and have big imaginations. They are strong willed, idealistic, ambitious, tolerant, and charming. They like people and so they have lots of friends. They also like collecting things.

Ox: 1925, 1937, 1949, 1961, 1973, 1985, 1997, 2009, 2021, 2033
Oxen like to be leaders. They are hardworking, dependable, sociable, patient, and honest. Oxen can be artistic and love being outside in nature.

Tiger: 1926, 1938, 1950, 1962, 1974, 1986, 1998, 2010, 2022, 2034
Tigers are brave and like adventure. They are determined, courageous, generous, sympathetic, and also like joking around. Tigers can be lucky with money.

Rabbit: 1927, 1939, 1951, 1963, 1975, 1987, 1999, 2011, 2023, 2035
Out of all the animal signs, Rabbits make the best friends. This is because they are peace-loving creatures. They are happy, gifted, ambitious, virtuous, and thoughtful and are attracted to beautiful things.

Dragon: 1928, 1940, 1952, 1964, 1976, 1988, 2000, 2012, 2024, 2036
Dragons are natural leaders with strong personalities. They have lots of energy and are full of bright ideas. They are passionate, vibrant, and brave and like to be in the middle of the action.

Snake: 1929, 1941, 1953, 1965, 1977, 1989, 2001, 2013, 2025, 2037
Snakes are wise and innovative. They are also patient, philosophical, and diplomatic. They have good imaginations and can be artistic. Snakes like to laugh and make other people laugh with them.

Horse: 1930, 1942, 1954, 1966, 1978, 1990, 2002, 2014, 2026, 2038
Horses are funny, popular, fearless, and hardworking. They like playing sports because
they have lots of energy. They are also confident, spirited, honest, sensitive, and brave.
Horses like helping others.

Goat: 1931, 1943, 1955, 1967, 1979, 1991, 2003, 2015, 2027, 2039
Goats are peaceful, friendly, gentle, and easygoing. They have good imaginations and love
anything artistic. They are also sensitive, modest, creative, and generous.

Monkey: 1932, 1944, 1956, 1968, 1980, 1992, 2004, 2016, 2028, 2040
Monkeys are very clever and gifted in everything they do. They are mischievous,
funny, reliable, inventive, and honest, and they like being with people.

Rooster: 1933, 1945, 1957, 1969, 1981, 1993, 2005, 2017, 2029, 2041
Roosters are easygoing and never shy. They like reading and traveling, so they
are very knowledgeable. They also have good memories and are brave,
resilient, independent, and lucky.

Dog: 1934, 1946, 1958, 1970, 1982, 1994, 2006, 2018, 2030, 2042
Dogs are faithful, loyal, and unselfish. They are steady workers, dependable,
patient, modest, intelligent, and caring. They make great friends because
they will always stand by you.

Pig: 1935, 1947, 1959, 1971, 1983, 1995, 2007, 2019, 2031, 2043
Pigs always try to do what is right. They are popular and tolerant and great fun to be with.
They are peace-loving, lucky, honest, and patient and also love their food.

*(Because the Chinese zodiac is based on a lunar calendar, birthdays in January
and early February will usually fall in the previous year's zodiac sign.
Consult a Chinese calendar for the specific years in question.)*